Dear Me!

Written and illustrated by
Marie Burlington

THE O'BRIEN PRESS
DUBLIN

First published 2006 by The O'Brien Press Ltd.,
12 Terenure Road East, Rathgar, Dublin 6, Ireland.
Tel: +353 1 4923333; Fax: +353 1 4922777
E-mail: books@obrien.ie
Website: www.obrien.ie

ISBN-10: 0-86278-976-1
ISBN-13: 978-0-86278-976-3

British Library Cataloguing in Publication Data
Burlington, Marie
Dear me!
1. Grandparent and child - Juvenile fiction 2. Children's stories
I. Title
823.9'2[J]

1 2 3 4 5 6 7 8 9 10
06 07 08 09 10

The O'Brien Press receives
assistance from

Printing: Bercker, Germany

Dear Me!

3

MARIE BURLINGTON has written and illustrated two books for younger readers, *Helpful Hannah* and *Lighthouse Joey* in the Panda series, and illustrated *Trouble for Tuffy* in the Flyers series.

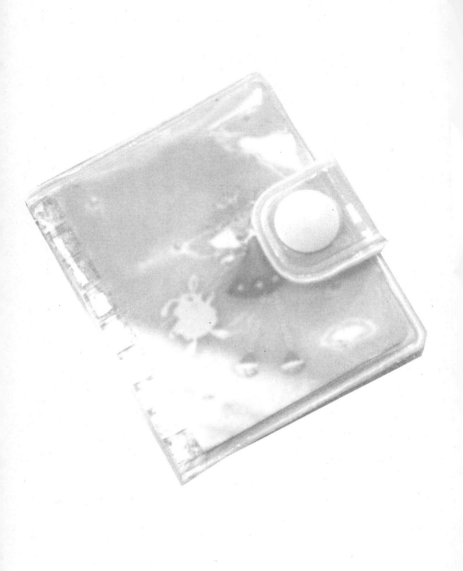

Saturday

Dear Me,

Good old Grandad, he's got some
great ideas. He could see that I was
bored silly and told me it might be
a good idea if I tried to keep a
diary. It really is a good idea,
because I have nothing to do all
day. I've come to live with him
because Mum's in hospital. I haven't been
here long and I have no one to play
with. His television has only a
few useless channels and he
doesn't even have a DVD
player. Since I arrived here
my day is like one long

big yawn

yawn that never ends. I didn't expect to spend the last few weeks of summer here.

My friend Tracy lives near me and Mum and she's wild. We do lots of things together and play in each others' houses all the time. I don't know anyone here, wild or tame. What's more my new school starts next week. I think when that day comes I'll have to develop the flu or mumps or some illness that's so catching they'll send me home straight away.

← me with mumps

It's okay here because Grandad is really kind. He's sort of crumpled and reminds me of an old cardigan. He likes to read newspapers a lot. Sometimes he falls asleep

grandad

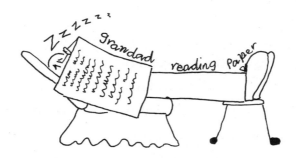

with them over his face and they go up and
down as he snores, which is really funny to
look at. I have to make sure that I giggle
under my breath or I might wake him up.
My Mum likes newspapers
too. She always does the
crosswords.

The day she went to
hospital it looked like she got
stuck on a clue she just
couldn't find the word for. She had this sort
of puzzled look on her face and she was
looking into space and mumbling to herself

← mum

about things. She must
have been thinking
really hard about it
because she didn't get the
dinner and she just sat there.
Eventually it was getting dark
and I got worried about
her and phoned my Aunt
Gemma. She came round
immediately and called the
doctor. He told us not to
worry and all she needed was some TLC.

← aunt gemma

He said that a few weeks in hospital
would have her back to normal in
no time. Normal is NOT a word
I'd use around Mum in the last
while. She's sort of got lost in her
own little world. She
seems kind of sad and I

10

haven't heard her laugh for so long I've forgotten what it sounds like.

Anyway, I got so bored here I started to talk to myself in the mirror. It's not such a bad idea when there's no one else to talk to! A mirror can tell you lots of things about yourself. It can tell you when you're happy and when you're sad. It can tell you when you look tired or ill. It can tell when you look cool and advise you how to do your hair and clothes and stuff like that. It's quite nice talking to my mirror me and it's quite nice writing to me. There's nothing much else to do here anyway so I might as well. Though I know if anyone sees me they'll think I've gone bananas.

Sunday

Dear Me,
I love this diary that
Grandad gave me
yesterday. I was
looking for something to
write in and he found this in one of his
cupboards. It has a bound cover and looks
like the kind of books you see in libraries,
but in this one the pages are blank like a
notebook. Mum calls Grandad a wise old
owl. He certainly looks like one with his big

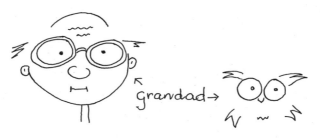

grandad→

glasses. He doesn't say a lot, but when he does say something it makes you think about things and how you look at them. He has wise sayings that he uses now and again and he sometimes gets a fit of laughing. For instance, when we

were having lunch the other day I asked him where my dad had gone and he told me that Dad had flown off somewhere. I was thinking that Grandad made Dad sound like some crazy bird, flapping about the place and flying off in a hurry. Grandad nearly fell off his chair laughing. 'Exactly', he said. 'That's exactly what he is.'

Anyway he thought it was hilarious. I didn't think it was hilarious at all because that's when Mum started to get really quiet and worried about things. I said to Grandad that I didn't think it was *that* funny and he said 'No, Button, you're absolutely right, it certainly isn't funny at all.'

Grandad calls me Button because I've got

← me

nose like button.

a nose like a button, but most people call me Cathy, which is my real name. That's

what Mum calls me. The doctor told us that
Mum will be better again soon. I have a
joke book and I go in and tell her a joke
every so often and I know some time soon
she'll find that clue she's been looking for
and she'll laugh at my jokes.

Q. Why do bees hum?
A. because They can't remember the words

Monday

Dear Me,

Grandad took me to town and bought me some clothes for school. That's the one cool thing about this new school – no uniforms, HURRAY! Grandad told me he's lost touch with fashion, so he let me buy whatever I wanted, which was great as Mum would never let me off so lightly. I got some jeans and some t-shirts and some new shoes and things. The colours are really cool. I got a belt with flowers and a bag too. I even got a hat with sparkly stars on it. Grandad said I looked like the bees knees. I didn't know bees had knees.

bees knees

Grandad told me that my cousin Tommy is coming to stay for a while as Aunt Gemma has to go away for her job. Mum says that Aunt Gemma is very dynamic (I'll have to look that up). She works in magazines. Tommy is two years younger than me and is always up to something. I'll have to think of somewhere to hide my diary as I'm sure he'll try to read it. I call him Tommy Tornado because he blows

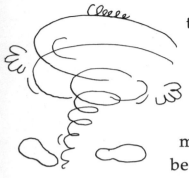

through the house and everything flies about when he passes. I might find a code or something that will make it difficult for him because if I know Tommy he'll be into everything in my room before I get a chance to stop him. It might be fun to have him around though, as even my mirror me is starting to get boring.

Anyway he should liven up the place a bit. Poor old Grandad has started putting the china in cupboards and locking up anything sharp.

I'm afraid he knows Tommy better than I do.

Tommy →

DYNAMIC = ENERGETIC, AMBITIOUS.

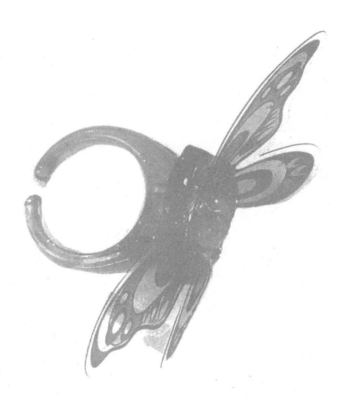

Tuesday

Dear Me,
Today I spent some time in the garden. Grandad

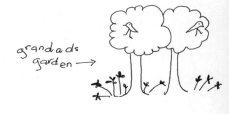

grandads garden →

has a fun garden and there are lots of places to sit so you can follow the sun all day. The house beside Grandad has a really untidy garden. It would be great to play in because there'd be lots of

places to hide. Mrs Hughes lives there, Grandad says she's a bit eccentric. I forgot to ask him what that means. I think she might be a bit dippy or something like that, but I'll look it up later. I had to get a ladder and climb halfway up to see into her garden.

I could make out an old garage with a big old car sticking out of it. Then I thought I saw her looking through the kitchen window and I got such a fright I nearly fell off the ladder.

I started to think about Mum when we came back from visiting her and I decided to ask Grandad about things.

'What's wrong with Mum, Grandad?' I asked.

Grandad looked a bit surprised and he stopped to think for a while. Then he

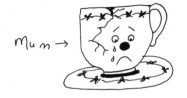

Mum →

looked at me over his glasses.

'You know, Button,' he said 'People are a bit like cups. There are big, sturdy mugs that you can't break and there are delicate, pretty china ones that are very fragile. Your mum is like a delicate, pretty china one. They break easily, but when they are mended properly they are just as good as new.'

I was wondering if this medicine called TLC that the doctor mentioned would do the trick so I asked him.

'Yes,' said Grandad, smiling. 'TLC is just the medicine she needs at the moment.'

I looked up eccentric.

ECCENTRIC = ODD

Wednesday

Dear Me,

Tommy arrived this morning. Boy, did he make a racket! He was like a *real* tornado knocking on the door! I could hear Grandad saying 'Oh, God!' under his breath. Poor Grandad looked like he was facing into a storm he couldn't get away from.

'Hello Curly,' he said to Tommy. (He calls him Curly because of his curly hair, the way he calls me Button because of my nose.)

← Curly

button nose →

'Hi Grandad, Hi Cathy!' shouted Tommy. Tommy doesn't talk, he shouts instead.

He had lots of bags and a suitcase and *all* his space toys. I only had time to pack a few clothes before Mum went into hospital so it would be good to have something to play with again.

Aunt Gemma went off with lots of hugs and kisses and a look of relief on her face. I hope she and Mum buy Grandad a big present after all this because I think he's going to need one. We had baked beans on toast for

beans on toast

lunch because that's Tommy's favourite food and in the afternoon we played astronauts and Star Wars and I was Princess Leia and he was Luke Skywalker and we saved the universe from all the baddies and lived happily ever after. After tea I found him under my bed.

my
o o° ← marbles

'What are you doing there?' I asked.
'I'm looking for your marbles.'
'What?' I asked.

'I asked Grandad why you were talking to yourself in the mirror and he said you'd probably lost your marbles so I thought I'd help you find them.'

'Keep looking.' I said. 'Thanks a million, Grandad.'

Q. what do you call your favourite floor covering?

A. A carpet.

Friday

Dear Me,

I've had lots of fun since Tommy arrived. He's only been here two days, but he's really settled in! We went shopping for food today and then we played in the garden. It was great not to be bored, but Tommy is quite a handful and I have to try and keep an eye on him. He goes off on his own and I can't find him anywhere. He has

a little notebook he keeps in his pocket. He writes down car registrations and phone numbers in it. He's usually out on the road writing down the numbers of all the cars that are parked and the ones that pass the house. He never stops moving for one minute.

When we were in the garden he got the ladder and looked into Mrs Hughes's garden. He told me there are lots of apple trees down the back and we should go in tomorrow and try and get some windfalls.

'What are windfalls?' I asked. Tommy is an expert on useless information.

'They're the apples that fall on the ground so it won't be like stealing,' he

replied, looking at me as if I was
stupid. I wondered if that's what
people mean when they say
that someone is leading
you down the garden
path. Because I'm
really not sure
whether it's right or
wrong to take the apples. I'm not sure
what's right or wrong a lot of the time.
Mum says that if it doesn't hurt people then
it's probably okay. Mum wouldn't hurt a
fly. Then I thought about Dad and about
him going away and leaving like that.

I thought Grandad might be able to tell
me why he did it because he did a good
explanation of why Mum had broken like a
china cup that was still pretty and
everything.

the garden path.

This evening, when Tommy had fallen asleep on the sofa and Grandad was reading his newspaper as usual, I asked him.

'Why did Dad leave?' I said.

Grandad sighed a big sigh and looked at me over his glasses again. 'Well, it's like this, Button,' he said. 'Some men realise they're not Elvis Presley anymore and feel that life hasn't turned out as they hoped or expected. That's just what happened to your dad.' Grandad went back to reading his newspaper. I was as wise as ever. Who the hell is Elvis Presley?

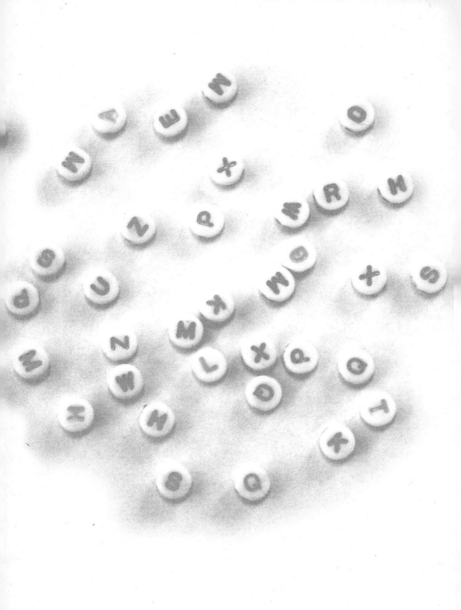

Sunday

(I had no time to write yesterday – there's no peace with Tommy here!)

Dear Me,

WHAT A DAY! Just the best ever! Tommy and I climbed into Mrs Hughes's garden and started to collect the windfalls. There were worms in some of them, but Tommy started eating them anyway. Then Mrs Hughes came out looking like a scarecrow from a nightmare and shouted, 'WHAT ARE YOU TWO AT?'

One of Grandad's sayings is that 'Honesty is the best policy', so I decided to tell the truth even though I was terrified.

'We're stealing your windfalls,' I said,

shaking all over, thinking that thieves must be the most terrified people in the world.

'Really,' she said. 'Imagine stealing from the birds! Oh well, I suppose it's alright, after all, they'd steal our food if they could.' I could see she was smiling so I didn't feel *too* bad.

'Ask your Grandad if you can come in and have some orange juice with the old lady next door.'

We ran in and asked Grandad. He said it was okay as long as we didn't break anything, so we went in and sat on the sofa. Everything about Mrs Hughes is faded. Her

← faded.

curtains, her chair covers, her clothes, herself, everything. It's like she's been sitting in the sunshine forever. We had orange juice and biscuits and then Tommy was looking at this machine and she told us it was a record player and asked us if we'd like to listen to some music. She showed us the records, which were like big, flat, black plates. They're called 'LPs', which means 'long-playing records'. She played one called 'Rock & Roll Dance Music'. Tommy started to dance as he can't sit still anyway and then Mrs Hughes started to dance. I felt a bit silly just sitting there so I started to dance as well! We danced and danced and laughed and laughed and Mrs Hughes said it would take her a week to recover.

Then I was looking at the records and I saw an Elvis Presley one and I thought, 'So

THAT'S who he is,' and I asked her to tell me about him. She told me he was a handsome singer who passed away and asked if I'd like to listen to the record. She put it on and he sang a song called 'Are you lonesome tonight?' The song was about people drifting apart. I got sad and couldn't help thinking about Mum and Dad

and the way they
drifted apart. I
could feel tears
bubbling up
like fizz in cola and
I looked at a picture on the
wall to try and distract myself.
Mrs Hughes was looking at me with her
kind face and I was really having a hard
time when Tommy fell off the back of the
sofa and we all started laughing again.

Monday

Dear Me,
Tommy spends his
life eating baked
beans and drinking
fizzy drinks and I'm
sure if he ate
something different
he wouldn't jump
around so much. His Mum works all the
time and they eat everything out of a
packet. We went in to see Mrs Hughes
again today and she showed us where she
grows vegetables, and there were lettuces
and radishes and spring onions and
tomatoes and lots of other things I don't

know the names of.
Tommy's eyes were out on
stalks, because he thinks
everything you eat comes
in a tin or a packet.

   She let him pick whatever
he wanted to eat and then
she made us a salad and
made a dressing by putting
oil and vinegar and herbs
in a jar and shaking them.
Tommy was really
unsure about the
food, but he ate it all up
anyway and tried to lick his
plate. I told him it was bad
manners, but he did it
anyway. Mrs Hughes
gave us some salad things

Tommy licking plate.

 to take home to Grandad, who just smiled and seemed really pleased with himself.

Salad dressing

1 part Olive Oil

3 Parts Vinegar (cider)

chopped fresh herbs

eg: parsley, mint, thyme, Coriander.

salt + pepper.

put in jar + shake well.

Dear Me,

I decided to design a crossword for Mum. I thought if I put all her favourite things in it she might remember that clue she's been stuck on. I was working on it all morning and then Grandad asked me to look for Tommy as he had one of his migraines coming on and he couldn't find him around the house.

I went out and looked in all the places I thought he might be. I even climbed up on the ladder and looked into Mrs Hughes's garden, but he was nowhere to be seen. I ran up and down the road calling out his name and then I started to get really worried. I didn't want to worry Grandad because migraines are really bad headaches and he needed to be quiet for it to get better. I was so worried my heart started to beat really loud and fast. I thought Mrs Hughes might be able to tell me what to do.

beat ~ beat ~ beat ~

'Come on in, Cathy. Let's see what we can do about the situation.' She gave me some lemonade and I started to calm down. Then she combed her hair and put on a jacket. 'I don't go out on search parties often,' she smiled, 'so I'd better tidy up a bit.' I noticed she looked rather nice when she tidied herself up.

'You don't look eccentric at all now,' I said, smiling at her. She just laughed her head off at that, though I wasn't sure why.

We looked everywhere and were just about to give up and think about disturbing Grandad and calling the police when Mrs Hughes remembered one last place. We made our way round the side of her house and there, sitting in her big, old car, was Tommy reading some comics he had found on the seat.

'You silly brat!' I yelled, 'You had us all worried sick!'

I was angry enough to shake him and happy enough to hug him at the same time.

'I was just getting the registration number of the car when I saw the comics,' he said, smiling one of his cheeky smiles and as usual we forgave him.

'Look,' he said. '*Incredible Hulk* comics, the really good ones from ages ago!'

I looked and they really did look old and a bit tired around the edges.

I noticed that Mrs Hughes looked a bit sad.

'Are you all right?' I asked. 'Those belonged to my son when he was little,' she said quietly.

'Where is he now?' I asked.

'He went to live far away a long time ago. I haven't seen him in such a long time.'

I held her hand for a little bit because I thought it might make her feel better and for a moment she looked like Mum, off in her own little world with no one but herself for company. I got her some lemonade and eventually she smiled at us both.

'Thank you, children,' she said at last. 'You've helped me a great deal.'

'No, thank you!' I said, 'I couldn't have found Tommy without you.'

'You can have those, Tommy,' she said.

'*Wow!*' said Tommy, '*Cool!*'

We went back into Grandad's house and he was still a bit unwell. I told him about

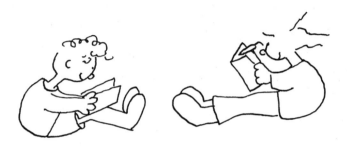

Mrs Hughes and everything and he just smiled and didn't say anything.

We spent the rest of the day quietly, for Grandad's sake. It was great because Tommy had the comics to keep him quiet and I could get on with designing the crossword.

Mum's Crossword.

Mum's favourite things.

ACROSS.

1. favourite place.
2. favourite meal.
3 favourite number.
4 favourite season.
5 favourite person.

down.

1. favourite hobby
2. favourite flower.
3 favourite weather.

Answers Across.

1. Sea
2. dinner.
3. ten.
4 Spring.
5. me.

Answers down.

1. gardening
2. Rose.
3. Snow.

Wednesday

Dear Me,
Grandad was much
better today. He decided
he should go and thank
Mrs Hughes for all her
kindness and for finding
Tommy. I suggested that he
bring her some flowers, so he sent me and
Tommy out to pick some in the garden. We
picked roses and daisies and dandelions
and anything that had a nice flower. We
wrapped them up in some gift paper we
found in a kitchen drawer. He spent about
half an hour in front of the mirror combing
his hair and considering he's nearly bald,

that's a lot of time! He looked like a real smarty-pants!

Smarty Pants.

Tommy and I giggled when he went out. He was gone for ages and ages and I was thinking we'd have to send out a search party for him too if he didn't come home soon. When he came home he was really delighted with himself and had a smile all over his face. Mrs Hughes had given him a jar of raspberry sauce to put on ice-cream, so we had two bowls each. I was thinking she should write a recipe book and it

would be especially good for Tommy because it would teach him that there's more to food than fizzy drinks and baked beans. Grandad told us that she had shown

him the car where we found Tommy and that it was a real beauty. It was an old classic car and he was going to help her do it up and we could help too.

Tomorrow I have to get ready for school because we go in on Friday for the morning to get our class places and sort out our books and things. I'm really dreading it. I told Grandad I thought I might have the flu or the mumps coming on and he fell around the place laughing again. Grandad thinks I'm some sort of comedian. He told me I'd have to come up with something better than that.

I left my mobile at home and I don't remember Tracy's number. It's a pity Tommy hasn't that number collected in his notebook. When Mum's better I'll ask her because she has them all written down somewhere. Anyway I'll have lots to tell Tracy when we meet up again.

Thursday

Dear Me,
HELP!! I found Tommy
reading my diary! I
chased him all around the
room. It was *really* hard to
catch him because he runs like
the wind! I'm not surprised with all
the baked beans. If
someone lit a match
behind him he'd go
off like a rocket.
They'd have to
send up the space
shuttle to get him
back to earth. No

wonder he wants to be an astronaut. I've decided to try and write in mirror code. So, from tomorrow on I'm going to write my diary in a way only my mirror me can read. Maybe it might be too much for Tommy to work out. He just wouldn't be able to sit still long enough. At least he's going home soon and I'll be able to write normally after that.

Since this is my last day of holidays Grandad took us out for the afternoon. We went to a café for lunch and then to the toy shop. He told us we could buy something each. Tommy bought a rocket with a little man inside and I bought this box of beads and hair clips. It's a pity Tracy's not around because we could do each other's hair. With this you have to divide the hair into little strands and put a bead at the top of the strand and then braid the strand and put a bead at the bottom. Then you have lots and lots of little plaits with beads at the top and bottom. I might ask Aunt Gemma or Mrs Hughes to help me.

Grandad had to go into an insurance place and ask about insuring Mrs Hughes car. It took ages and ages and it was really boring. They had a water cooler and Tommy had used up all the cups by the time we left. The people behind the

counters were starting to get very cross looking!

I got a few pens and things for school, but I'm trying not to think about it. We played space games with Tommy's rocket and he tried to put a bead in my hair and tried to braid it. It'll take me forever to get the tangles out. I tried writing in mirror writing, but it's too difficult. I'll just have to find a good hiding place.

tangle

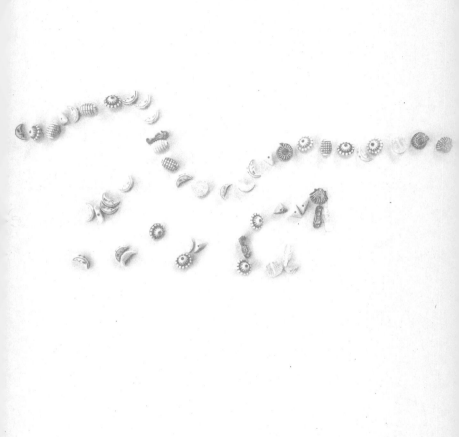

Friday

Dear Me,
Today I went to my
new school. I really
hated it. It was like
loads of huge shoe
boxes side by side.
Mum would say it had
no character. Places have to have nooks and
crannies to have character and there wasn't
a nook or a cranny
anywhere to be
seen. I was so
nervous my
butterflies had
butterflies. I was

there on my own and Miss Kelly the
teacher tried her best to look after me, but
she was too busy. I was thinking
that Grandad wasn't the
only one who had lost
touch with fashion as
lots of the girls were
wearing designer
clothes and some
even had make-up
on! I was thinking of Grandad's sayings
and one is about feeling like a fish out of
water, which is just the way I felt.

There was a girl who had a group of
friends and they kept looking over at me
and whispering and laughing. I was
thinking I might make a run for the door
when this girl came over and asked me if
I'd like to sit beside her. Her name was

Alice and she had freckles that looked like someone had spent forever painting on her face. She was really nice and I forgot about the other girls for a while. She told me to ignore them. 'They think they're important,' she said. 'That one,' she pointed to one of the girls while she wasn't looking, 'Is called Rea, the rest just follow her around. She bosses them and they act like they've no minds of their own. I just ignore them and they go away.'

Alice gave me a pen and some pages from her notebook, which had glitter on it. We got our

timetables and I put some books in my locker, but all I could think about was what Tracy was doing and why I had to go through all this in the first place.

I used to hate my old school, but it was nothing like this. At least I had Tracy. We always walked home together and had a good old moan about things. I could have told her about Mum.

I don't know Alice well enough to explain about Mum and everything, although I'm sure she'd understand. I'd really hate the other girls to find out about

Mum not being herself and about Dad leaving. I feel I'd like to wrap Mum up in cotton wool. I sometimes feel like that about Grandad too. He looks sort of old and tired sometimes, as if all our problems are a bit too much for him. I'd like to talk to him about school, but I think he has enough on his plate. I don't think he'd want me to be embarrassed about Mum being in hospital because he loves her so much. I can't really say anything because he mightn't understand why I'm worrying at all. Sometimes I just give him a big smile because I want him to feel better.

This new school is a bit different. It smells different to my other school and all the places and routines are different too. I'm finding it all strange and I feel a bit scared. Then I worry about Mum. I really need her to mind me, but I have to mind her instead, which isn't fair. If that girl Rea found out about her I'm sure she'd really have a go at me. I cringe when I think of them all standing there laughing at me and then I want to cry when I think they might laugh at Mum. It's not as if she doesn't have enough to deal with, feeling as helpless as she does.

She reminds me of a time when I was on the beach and had spent the whole afternoon building all these lovely sand castles. Then one huge wave washed them all away, in one big go. It's as if everything she worked hard to build has been wasted and all the lovely dreams and ideas that went with all that effort have been wasted as well. I just sat there not knowing what to do next, just the way Mum does now. I know Mum will get better, I just wish it was soon. Please, Mum, make it soon.

Alice

Saturday

Dear Me,
I found a new place to hide my diary that Tommy can't reach (on top of the wardrobe), so I don't have to try to write in mirror writing any more.

← hiding place

*   *   *

Did you know that miracles sometimes happen when you least expect them?

Well, this is what happened today. Grandad and Tommy were going over to

Mrs Hughes to clean her car. The car used to belong to her son and when he moved away she didn't sell it because it reminded her of him. So it just sat there and sat there. Grandad said we'd all go on a picnic when it's cleaned up and he's had a chance to get the engine going. Anyway, he told me I could spend a few hours with Mum on my own to catch up with things. I was thinking that a few minutes would be enough because Mum isn't that easy to talk to these days. I had the crossword to give her and I thought I'd show her my hair beads. Anything but talk about school!

Grandad went off with Tommy and left me in the room with her. I was looking out the window and thinking how pretty the view was and how I bet she hadn't even noticed it. Then I started to tell her about things. About Mrs Hughes and her son and Grandad's headache and Tommy and Alice and all the things that had happened since she went into hospital. I put the crossword down in front of her and she just looked at it. Then I took out the beads and told her about them. I was just thinking that my life was like a shopping basket and that Grandad and Tommy and school and everything were like packets in the

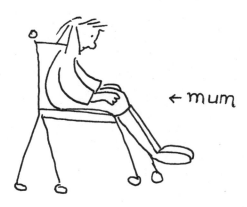

← mum

shopping basket and that the basket was getting too heavy for me to carry. I was really sick of talking to her and getting so little reaction. Just then I opened the box of beads and they fell all over the floor! Then I thought I'd had enough and I started to cry because I was really, really angry about everything and I kicked the beads all over the place and ran out of the room.

I was standing in
the corridor leaning
against the wall and
being really upset
when a nurse came and brought me back to
Mum. And guess what? She was picking up
the beads and putting them back in the
packet. The nurse told me to sit down and
she gave Mum a comb and

guess what again, Mum
started combing my
hair and putting the
beads in! I just sat there
quietly for hours and
Mum did all my hair and
when she finished I turned
around and she smiled and
it was like a big, beautiful flower opening
up in front of me and I hugged her and

hugged her until my arms hurt and I said, 'Oh, Mum!' and I asked her if she had found that clue she had been looking for and she

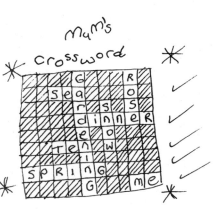

nodded and said 'Yes.' Then she looked at my crossword and she did that too. Afterwards I ran to Grandad in the car park and told him what had happened and he just said 'Good girl, Button, good girl.'

Sunday

Dear Me,
I said that miracles can happen and I
wasn't wrong. The doctor
phone Grandad and told
him that Mum was on
the mend and would be
home soon! Grandad
had a smile on his face all
day and he and Tommy

brought me over to see the car. It looked
really beautiful and sparkled in the sun.
Mrs Hughes said we can all go for a picnic
when Mum comes home. Tommy showed
me where he had shone up all the hubcaps
himself. He was very proud of all his hard

work. I patted him on the back and told him he was the greatest. He told me he liked my hair with all the beads in it, he said I looked cool. We had lunch in Mrs Hughes's garden, which is full of nooks and crannies. I drew a picture of it and this is what it looks like.

Tommy had to go home this evening. Aunt Gemma had just come in from the airport and she was all hustle and bustle. I told her I had collected some of Mrs Hughes's recipes that Tommy likes. I said he shouldn't eat baked beans all the time. She told me I was getting bossy just like my Mum, and then she laughed and said she'd

try out the recipes. I really miss Tommy already. I couldn't talk to my mirror me when he was around because he always stood behind me and made faces. So now I can talk happily to myself whenever I want. Though it's been so busy around here I just haven't had the time.

Tuesday

Dear Me,

Sorry I didn't write yesterday! Well, I don't have to hide my diary any more because Tommy's gone home. He's coming over on the day we're all going on the picnic. School was a bit better so far this week. Miss Kelly saw Rea whispering and laughing at me and she made her sit on the other side of the class on her own. She told her if she keeps it up she can stay on her own all year. Rea had a face like a wet Monday. (One of Grandad's sayings.) During our break I took some of my beads

beads

Alice

out and put them in Alice's hair. I'm starting to get a bit more used to the place now,

I Miss Tracy

me.

but I still miss Tracy.

I must say I'm glad Alice made friends with me. She helps me with everything and she's introduced me to her friends, Emma and Ciara. They showed me where the big hall is; we're going to put on a play at the end of the year and they think I should try out for a part. We didn't have plays in my old school so that might be a bit of fun. Alice got up on the stage and started to sing. She was pretending to be a famous pop singer. She called me up on stage, 'Come on, Cathy!' We all got up and sang a silly pop song. I hope no one saw us! I must say it was a good laugh.

Alice brought me around the school as if she was one of those estate agents selling a house. 'This is the teachers' room,' she said in a pretend posh voice, 'Notice the luxury compared with the classrooms.' She had a pretend serious face on too. 'This is the broom cupboard,' she said, 'Notice the luxury compared with the classrooms.' Yes, Alice is a laugh all right! She's just the ticket for a new girl in a new school.

All the girls play lots of sport in this school. I'm not too good at sports although I'm quite a fast runner. I might practise with Alice and see if I can get up a bit of speed. It would be great for Grandad and Mum if I won a race. I'd be really proud if they came to watch me.

Friday

Dear Me,
SURPRISE, SURPRISE!! I came home from school after my first full week there and guess who opened the door? It was Mum! She gave me the biggest hug ever. She

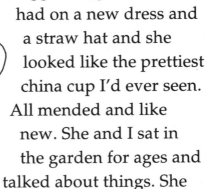

had on a new dress and a straw hat and she looked like the prettiest china cup I'd ever seen. All mended and like new. She and I sat in the garden for ages and talked about things. She told me she felt like she had been in a long, dark tunnel without any light. I asked

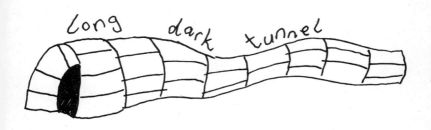

long dark tunnel

her if that medicine TLC had done the trick
and she agreed it was the best medicine
and told me we all need lots of it. Grandad
was over in Mrs Hughes's house. Mum was
doing some weeding so I said I'd help. We
decided to take the weeds off the big, old
wall between the houses. Mum got up on a
chair and I got the ladder.

We were just getting started on the
weeds when we heard some music. Mum
said it was a waltz. We looked
over and there were
Grandad and Mrs
Hughes dancing in
the sitting room to the
music from her

record player. For a moment we stopped and watched as Grandad and Mrs Hughes danced round in circles. It looked like a little piece of magic where time stood still and no one was old or young or anything like that. Mum told me later that's what happiness is about, when you don't have any ideas about things and you just enjoy something for what it is. She said that it was a special memory I could fold up and put in my pocket of memories.

I think Mum is turning into a wise old owl just like Grandad.

Friday

Dear Me,

Wow! I haven't written for a whole week! I haven't had a chance because so many things are happening.

Today everyone got off school early and so we decided it would be a good day to go on our picnic. Tommy came over and gave Mum a big hug and got jam on her new dress, but she didn't mind. Grandad sat us

all in the car and off we went. The car looked beautiful and shiny and lots of people turned and looked at it. We were half way through town when I spotted Rea and her friends. She kept staring at us and her mouth was open so wide she

could have caught a hundred flies. Tommy stuck out his tongue. I told him it was bad manners, but he did it anyway.

According to Grandad the old car purred like a kitten. We drove down to the sea.

Grandad took off his shoes and went for a paddle with us. Tommy and I splashed

him and he got really wet, but being
Grandad he just laughed and splashed us
back. Mum and Mrs Hughes are talking
about putting a recipe book
together because they're
both really good cooks.
They were quite busy
sitting there making
their plans.

Tonight I
phoned Tracy.
We talked for
ages and ages.
She's going to
come and stay
next weekend. She hates being back at
school too. It's great to be in touch with her
again. It's great because I don't feel lonely
anymore. Everything is getting back to

normal again and some of the changes that have happened are really nice. When we were at the sea Grandad and Mrs Hughes went off to get some ice-creams for us. I said to Mum that we should get Grandad a present. Mum just looked at them as they walked down the beach.

'I think you've already given him one,' she said. I guess she meant that Mrs Hughes was the best present anyone could have and she was right.

Thursday

Dear Me,
Sorry Diary, I haven't written for nearly a week, and I haven't had a chance to talk to mirror me for *ages*. It's just that it's getting to be a bit too busy around here. Even Grandad has stopped reading the paper all day and Mum hasn't looked at a crossword since she did the one I made for her. First of all we have to go back and collect all our things in our old house because Mum told me that she and Dad want to sell it. I don't mind because Grandad's house has always felt like home anyway and we don't need two houses. Mum says it's time to move on and have new adventures in our lives. I'll

be glad to have all my old toys and clothes around me at last.

some of my toys

scRabble

Tommy calls to see Grandad really often so we can do lots of things together and Aunt Gemma knows someone who might be interested in that recipe book Mrs Hughes and Mum are planning to write.

Earlier today Mum and I were in the kitchen tidying up and she swept under the press.

'What's this?' she asked. It

was Tommy's notebook with all his numbers. I looked at it and pointed out the car numbers and phone numbers.

'Look!' I said, looking at the last number he had written in his notebook. 'This one looks like Mrs Hughes's son. Tommy must have copied it down when we were in her house.' It said, 'Paul, New York' and it had a big long number beside it. I told Mum about Mrs Hughes looking all sad and everything when Tommy found the comics. Mum looked like she had just had a brainwave.

'Wait here,' she said, sounding all excited and taking the notebook with her.

She went into the hall and was talking on the phone for ages. When she came back she told me that she had had some nice surprises since she came home. Now it was time for someone else to have one. I forgot all about it, but next thing Mrs Hughes came in and was jumping up and down. She was all excited because her son had phoned her and he's going to come and visit her next year. Mum just winked at me and I winked back. We were all jumping up

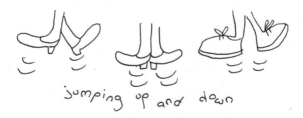

jumping up and down

and down and clapping our hands when

Grandad came in and said he must be in the wrong house and pretended to walk out again. I had to go and grab him and get him back. He says we must have eaten jumping beans in the soup we had for lunch. Either that or he'll have to get Tommy back to collect all the marbles we've lost. Grandad is really funny sometimes. I told him he was the best Grandad ever and he patted me on the head and told me to find some mischief to get myself into.

All in all it's turned out to be a really interesting summer in the end. I have to go now and get my room tidied before Tracy comes to stay. Mrs Hughes has invited us to tea on Sunday and she wants to know

what Tracy likes to
eat. If I know Tracy
she'll eat everything,
plate and all.

Oh, by the way, I was at the chemist
getting some bandages for Tommy because
he's always falling and cutting himself and
I asked the chemist if she'd ever heard of a
medicine called TLC. She told me it was the
best and most important medicine that ever
existed. I'll look it up and check what
it is before I finish writing
tonight.

I'll have lots to tell you next
time. Bye for now.
TLC=TENDER LOVING
CARE